Angelina on Stage

To my wonderful mother   KH

To my father, Edward Craig, with love   HC

PUFFIN BOOKS

Published by the Penguin Group
Penguin Books Ltd, 80 Strand, London WC2R 0RL, England
Penguin Group (USA), Inc., 375 Hudson Street, New York, New York 10014, USA
Penguin Books Australia Ltd, 250 Camberwell Road, Camberwell, Victoria 3124, Australia
Penguin Books Canada Ltd, 10 Alcorn Avenue, Toronto, Ontario, Canada M4V 3B2
Penguin Books India (P) Ltd, 11 Community Centre, Panchsheel Park, New Delhi – 110 017, India
Penguin Books (NZ) Ltd, Cnr Rosedale and Airborne Roads, Albany, Auckland, New Zealand
Penguin Books (South Africa) (Pty) Ltd, 24 Sturdee Avenue, Rosebank 2196, South Africa

Penguin Books Ltd, Registered Offices: 80 Strand, London WC2R 0RL, England

www.penguin.com

First published by Aurum Press Ltd 1986
Published by Viking 2001
1 3 5 7 9 10 8 6 4 2
Published in Puffin Books 2001
9 10

Printed in Italy by Printer Trento Srl

British Library Cataloguing in Publication Data
A CIP catalogue record for this book is available from the British Library

ISBN 0–670–91156–9 Hardback
ISBN 0–140–56866–2 Paperback

To find out more about Angelina, visit her web site at **www.angelinaballerina.com**

Angelina on Stage

Story by Katharine Holabird Illustrations by Helen Craig

PUFFIN BOOKS

Angelina's cousin Henry liked to go to her ballet lessons at Miss Lilly's and join in the dancing. Henry always followed close behind Angelina, copying her graceful steps, but he wiggled and wobbled and didn't look like a ballet dancer at all.

After each class, Angelina showed Henry the *right* way
to do the pliés and arabesques and twirls.

But Henry kept on dancing in his own funny way.

Then one day Miss Lilly received a letter from Mr Popoff, the great musical director. "Angelina," said her ballet teacher, "how would you like to be a magic fairy in a real grown-ups' ballet?" Angelina was thrilled. "Oh, yes!" she cried.

"It is called *The Gypsy Queen*," said Miss Lilly excitedly. Then she turned to Henry. "Mr Popoff needs a little elf too, and you are the perfect size."

"Hooray!" shouted Henry, but Angelina just crossed her fingers for good luck, hoping he wouldn't do anything too silly.

At rehearsals Angelina learned to fly through the air with a special wire attached to her costume so that she looked like a fairy floating down out of the sky. Henry was supposed to scamper through the woods below looking for the fairy, but he often got mixed up and went the wrong way.

All the actors and actresses adored Henry anyway, and during the breaks, the lovely Madame Zizi gave him little treats in her dressing room. Then Mr Popoff decided that Henry should say something on stage, and Angelina felt very jealous.

Everyone cheered when Henry came on stage and said in his little squeaky voice, "There goes my friend, the magic fairy!" But he was not so good at finding his way from the dressing room to the stage and was always getting lost.

On the night of the first
performance, everyone
backstage was very excited.
Angelina waited in the wings
with her crown on and her
wand ready as the audience
crowded into the theatre and
the orchestra began to play.
Madame Zizi glanced around
nervously and said, "Oh dear,
where's my little elf?"

Angelina ran wildly through the corridors looking for Henry …

… and bumped into him as he was running the wrong way down the hall. "I got lost again!" Henry sobbed as Angelina grabbed his hand and raced back to the stage.

Angelina had her special wire fastened just in time.
She soared up over the trees waving her magic
wand as Henry jumped out from the wings
and skipped through the woods to the
front of the stage.

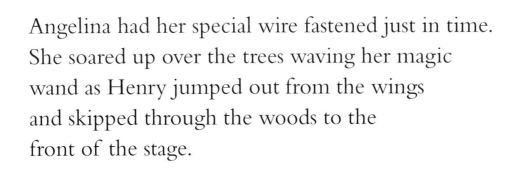

Henry turned and saw the theatre filled with lights and a sea of strange faces. He couldn't open his mouth. He just stared out at the audience.

For an awful moment nothing happened.

"Serves him right," thought Angelina, still feeling annoyed, but when she looked down and saw how terrified Henry looked, she felt sorry for him.

Angelina waved her magic wand and called to Henry in a loud, clear voice, "Hello, little elf, can you see me?"

Henry looked up with relief and said, "There goes my *best* friend, the magic fairy."

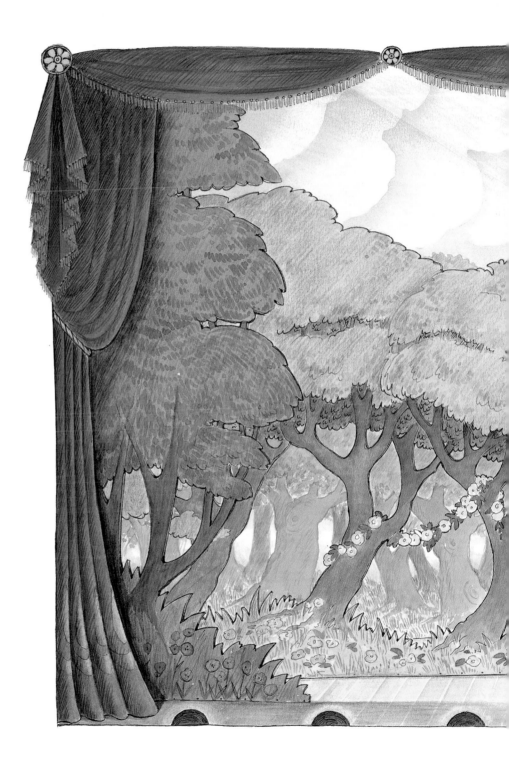

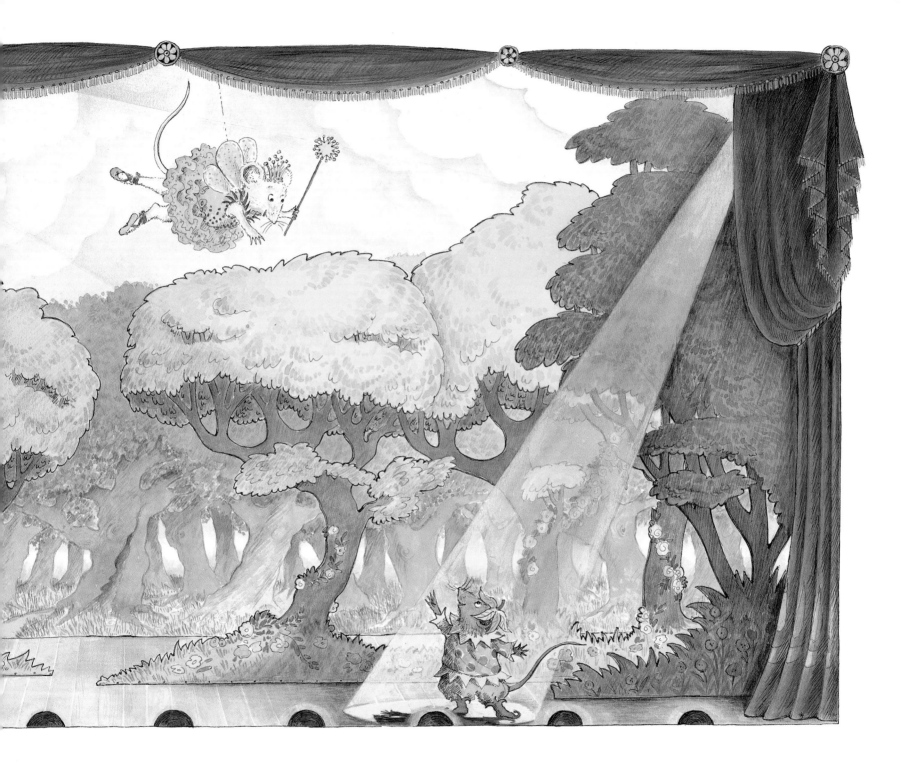

At the end of the show, Angelina and Henry took
a curtain call with all the actors and dancers.

The audience cheered and clapped, and the director
thanked everyone for a wonderful performance.

Madame Zizi gave Angelina some of her own roses, and Mr Popoff smiled at her and said, "You're a fine actress, and you'll have a speaking part too, from now on."

Angelina was so pleased that she took Henry by the hands and waltzed around the stage with him until they were both very dizzy.